For little mice everywhere - David
For Lydia Scarlett - Ruth

00-1026 Ingram 11-17-00 $14.95/8.52

Copyright © 1999 by David Ellwand
First published in Great Britain by Templar Publishing
Published by Lothrop, Lee & Shepard Books
a division of HarperCollins*Publishers*
1350 Avenue of the Americas, New York, NY 10019
www.harpercollins.com
PRINTED IN BELGIUM
First U.S. edition published in 2000.

1 3 5 7 9 10 8 6 4 2

LIBRARY OF CONGRESS CATALOGING-IN-PUBLICATION DATA
Ellwand, David.
Midas Mouse/David & Ruth Ellwand; photographs by David Ellwand.
p. cm.
Summary: Midas Mouse becomes so enthralled with sunlight that he
is given the power to turn anything he touches into gold.
ISBN 0-688-16745-4
[1. Mice—Fiction. 2. Gold—Fiction.] I. Ellwand, Ruth. II. Title.
PZ7.E4785Mi 2000 [E]—DC21 98-44728 CIP AC

Midas Mouse

BY DAVID AND RUTH ELLWAND

Photographs by David Ellwand

Lothrop, Lee & Shepard Books
A division of HarperCollins*Publishers*

*M*idas Mouse lived in the dark. By day he curled up with his brothers and sisters in the mousehole behind the kitchen wall. At night he scampered through the dark kitchen, feasting on tasty crumbs and cookies and cheese.

"Daylight is dangerous for mice," his mother warned her children. But Midas had seen the sunbeams lighting up the room beyond the baseboard, and he longed to play in them.

One day as he watched the dust dance in the sunlight through a crack in the floorboards, Midas forgot his mother's warning. He slipped out of the mousehole and into the light. The sun was warm and dazzling. It sparkled on his fur like gold dust. It lay on the floor in golden puddles.

Midas closed his eyes to the glare and danced until he was dizzy. "Oh," he sighed, spinning in a sunbeam, "I wish *I* were like the sun. I wish everything *I* touched would turn to gold."

*F*or a moment, his fur felt as warm as if the sun itself

had touched him with one golden finger.

$\mathcal{T}$hen he scurried back to the mousehole,

his feet filled with a strange tingling.

"Come out and play in the sun,"

he called to his brother Freddy.

But Freddy would not budge from the mousehole.

"You have changed, Midas," he squeaked.

"Whatever have you done?"

I have been touched by the sun,"

said Midas. And sure enough,

as he ran back out across the floorboards,

he knew that his wish had been granted.

*E*verything he touched

    with his four pink paws

        suddenly turned to hard, shiny gold.

*H*e ran over the books on the dusty des

till their covers sparkled

and their pages shimmere

*H*e danced onto the hall clock and turned its key to shiny gold.

*H*e scampered through the kitchen,

turning crumbs to gold dust.

*T*hen he ran up and down the strings of an old violin.

"I can make music!" he cried. But as his feet touched them,

the golden strings grew silent.

It doesn't take music, though,

to wake a cat!

*B*ut Midas was not afraid. Up the cat's legs he ran, then down its black back, till soon the cat was no more than a shiny statue, crouching silently in the sunlight.

*N*ow Midas could run anywhere he pleased. Up and

down, all over the house, he turned everything into gold:

dishes and doormats, cups and cushions, even the cheese.

$\mathcal{M}$idas's mother slipped out of the mousehole and blinked in the glare of the golden room.

"Look, Mother!" sang Midas. "I am like the sun. I have turned everything to gold!"

But his mother only shook her head sadly. "Oh, Midas," she said, "what shall we do now, for we cannot eat golden cheese or golden bread crumbs. We will surely starve."

Midas nibbled at a crumb.

It was as hard as a pebble.

What *have* I done? he thought

as the sun set outside the windows

and long shadows crept across the floor.

Midas shivered.

How he wished that everything could be as it was before.

And as he wished with all his tiny beating heart,

the pale moon rose in the dark sky.

It cast its magical light through the windows,

transforming everything in its silvery glow.

The room was no longer made of gold,

and when the moonbeams fell on Midas,

he became just an ordinary mouse again.

*T*he cat stretched and yawned.

*M*idas scurried to the safety of the mousehole.

Then, while the other mice feasted on tasty

tidbits and played in the dark, Midas curled up

and slept, chasing moonbeams in his dreams

through the long, cozy night.